I0741684

EYES OF WATER & STONE

From Havana with Love

CEDRIC BROWN

Thanks to those who supported me in this journey,
& to AMB for making it happen.
Y ahora se acabó.

Por el Mar de las Antillas...
navega Cuba en su mapa:
Un largo lagarto verde,
con ojos de piedra y agua.

In the sea of the Antilles...
Cuba straddles the map
a long green lizard
with eyes of stone and water.

from *Un largo lagarto verde*
Nicolás Guillén
1902-1989

I.

I couldn't keep my eyes off the gun. I wasn't afraid for myself, just for Félix.

After a six-month separation, Félix and I were finally reunited once I scraped together enough money to make the trip back to Havana to see him. After the first time we met, I couldn't forget his charm, his eyes, and maybe our shared desperation. So despite the miles and barriers between San Francisco and Havana, we'd bonded through letters and email. He conjured loving and romantic words from his delicious mouth for my ears only. Or so I thought. I was trying to figure out whether I loved him, or whether I loved his country. Both of them were simultaneously enchanting and hard-edged. Both of them led me back to fading crown jewel of the Caribbean.

That afternoon, Félix and I were strolling down the Malecón, Havana's famous seaside concourse. The four-laned Malecón winds along the northern shore of Havana, offering a panoramic view of the skyline and with the fabled Nacionál and Havana Libre hotels sitting on their respective hilltops. People amble along this mighty boulevard, hoping to be cooled by a breeze sweeping in from the Florida Straits, or by playful sea spray from the powerful waves pounding the rocks just beyond the Malecón wall. The social lives of Habañeros play out daily: tightly-knit groups of teens perform fierce free-flow raps to syncopated beats. A father and son cast fishing lines into the rough tide. A lone couple gazes off across the waters towards La Yuma, the United States, which lies just 90 miles to the north.

Félix and I walked slowly, re-acquainting ourselves with each other and making small talk. A machine gun-toting man shattered our peaceful stroll looming over us dressed in the dark blue militia jumpsuit and epaulettes of the policía. *"Identificácion. Dámelo."*

He first aimed his order at Félix, who had already reached into his pocket to pull out the always-required ID card. Félix handed it to the policeman, who scrutinized it with a scowl and flicked it back in Félix's direction. Every time the officer moved his arm, the machine gun draped over his shoulder jerked like a nervous tic.

He looked at me next. I don't remember whether he demanded my ID using the respectful *ustéd* or the informal and condescending *tu*, but his aggression didn't surprise me. Black folks catch hell from the police in every corner of the globe. Nevertheless, showing the confidence – well, muted arrogance that the privilege of U.S. citizenship can bring while abroad, I handed him my California driver's license. My passport was securely locked away in my hotel room safe. The officer's sandy white face twitched with displeasure as he looked at both sides of the license.

"What is this?" He demanded.

"My identity card."

"Where is your passport?"

"In the hotel."

"Which hotel?"

I didn't want to endanger Félix by further annoying the officer with a too-slow response, so I tried to get my muddled Spanish together in order to finish this interruption of our crime-in-progress – walking down the Malecón.

"Mélia Cohiba."

"Where are you from?"

"California." Like my license says. It translates directly, you fuckin' idiot.

"Where are your parents from?" I was surprised by that question.

"The United States." Gotcha.

"How do you know each other?"

"We're friends," Félix offered, putting forward a brave face in front of the posturing policeman.

"How do you know each other?" Officer Friendly repeated, twitching again. The picture was clear to us all. He'd caught himself two *maricónes*.

"We met here in Havana," Félix continued, curtly.

"*Ah, ¿Sí?* Well, what's his last name?" He threw out this zinger, no doubt hoping to catch me in a lie.

"Meléndez," I countered with the confidence of a man who'd gone to bed for six months repeating the same name in his prayers. "Félix Meléndez Teller," adding his mother's family name for good measure.

Satisfied that he'd made us sweat enough for one afternoon, the officer grunted and stalked off. Félix and I walked for a few minutes in painful silence. I immediately thought of my Miranda Rights and best friend at the ACLU. Instead, I was here with Félix, who explained that he unfortunately was used to such harassment, and the fact that he was walking with a tourist could've earned him a fine or a trip to jail. Fortunately I'd remembered his name, he joked sadly.

Bienvenidos a Cuba. Despite the ever-present faces of pop idol revolutionaries, free-flowing rum, and sizzling rhumba, I was standing in a police state. Nice reminder, just in case I forgot.

CUBA
contra el terrorismo
y contra la guerra

II.

I ended up in Cuba on a whim. Jake, one of my best friends, asked me to travel there as his photography assistant while he captured images of the classic Spanish colonial architecture in Habana Vieja now preserved and cherished as a UN World Heritage Site. This was one of the few ways (however dubious) that a U.S. citizen could travel there legally at the time, given the cumbersome politics of the tired blockade in effect since 1962. I had enough Spanish language proficiency, developed over years of classes from junior high school through college, for Jake to consider me as a useful sidekick and novice translator.

When I first told my mother that I was preparing to go, her lyrical and light "Ahhh, Cuuuba!" – no doubt accompanied by images of palm trees, conga drums, and cigars – was followed by a pause and "Now why do you want to go *there*?" I don't have any ancestral or family ties to the island, but I've always felt connected to it, this ominous paradise, AK-47s and fatigues among lush mountains and cane fields.

Cuba had occupied a place in my mind for a long time. I knew that something serious had gone down there, a revolution that greatly intensified the nuclear anxiety of the Cold War. *El lagarto verde*, the green lizard of an island, according to national poet Nicolás Guillén, looked to its northern neighbor and said *"No tenemos ningún miedo de ti"* – we're not afraid of you! I remembered reruns of *I Love Lucy* and Desi Arnaz playing the raven-haired and heavy-accented Ricky Ricardo. I remembered hearing about the warm reception that black Americans gave Fidel Castro at the Theresa Hotel in Harlem after he was treated rudely by white people downtown. I remembered being afraid of the Marielitos after reading that Castro had put hardened criminals and "retards" on the boats, even though my hometown was a two-day drive from their south Florida landing place. I remembered a photo in *Ebony* magazine of a white factory worker with the caption that said "U.S. immigration policy favors Cubans over Haitians, as most Cuban workers are white." I remembered the giant Alberto Juantorena's brown Afro framing his bobbing, twisting head as he ran to two gold medals in the 1976 Summer Olympics in Montréal. I remembered learning the words to Guantanamera in the seventh grade, and thought for years that it was a Mexican party song.

A co-worker who later became a good friend provided my first glimpse into the lives of real Cubans – well, the Miami-based version. I would barrage her with questions until well after the end of the workday. She was born in the United States to parents who'd left Cuba around the time of the Revolution. She spoke of Christmases with a roasted pig and arroz con leche, and sipping café cubano in Little Havana. I'd sneak by her desk to hear her speaking impossibly speedy Spanish on the phone with her parents or sisters. Her father, a physician, had vowed never to return to his home while Castro was in power. He died without ever seeing Cuba again.

I met another woman who self-identified as Afro-Cuban. This struck me in a profound way, as though she possessed some sort of deep-rooted spiritualism only a step removed from the Motherland. This connection, in my mind, gave her immense spiritual powers that her North American counterparts – black and white – would never be able to conjure. But this Afro-Cubana probably didn't have any more connection to a spiritual world than the average person, because for her being Afro-Cubana simply meant growing up with certain cadences, tastes, and politics. This fascinated me, and I wanted to learn more.

Jake and I arrived in Havana on a densely humid night, descending down the airplane steps onto the tarmac. We hustled past unsmiling immigration agents and customs officers who were even more grim-faced. I felt a twinge of "Uh oh."

After settling into our hotel, which was decent by our norteamericano standards, Jake and I walked down a hill toward a street celebration on the Malecón. I chuckled as I asked myself "Where am I, Detroit?" The crowd was nearly all black! When I say black, I mean those folks who would be claimed as black in the States, including mixed-race people, because racial identity there defies the U.S. one-drop rule. This brown-skinned spectrum allowed me to move around somewhat inconspicuously, a comfort my blonde, blue-eyed friend Jake did not have. On the flip side, during the trip he was afforded certain gestures not extended to me – in restaurants the check would come to him, he would be addressed first, and (in my opinion) people would respond to his questions first – and in English.

Maybe Jake and I were mistaken for another kind of couple. Havana seemed to be an international destination for exotic black flesh, despite Fidel Castro's attempts to stamp out sex tourism, or at least keep it on the down low. This battle with the world's oldest profession had strong roots in pre-Revolution conditions, where men from all over Europe and the Americas converged on the island to test the legendary libidos of Cuban women, and to a lesser degree, Cuban men. Fast forward 50 years, some of the young people - from the gorgeous to the decent-enough-looking - put their charms and bodies to work in the hopes of augmenting their access to a better life. So it comes as no surprise that the volatile combination of stereotypical Latin sensuality, the need for hard currency, and tourists' lust for brown flesh provides a fertile economic opportunity. It isn't exactly prostitution, since the dynamic is more than a simple exchange of sex for money or the exploitation of natives by tourists. The game is more about access – getting a nice dinner in a restaurant, enjoying an evening in a disco or club with an otherwise prohibitive cover charge, receiving nice gifts or a few dollars for posterity or the ultimate – being invited to visit or live abroad. I saw women working men, men working men, and men working women. Once while standing in the hotel lobby, I encountered a young woman who was determined to go wherever I was going that evening, even as I played dumb to what was happening. She finally broke it down for me in English: "Buy me!"

Before traveling to Havana, I had a chance to watch the stunning film *Soy Cuba*, a 1964 Soviet-produced documentary directed by Mikhail Kalatozov and written by Yevgeny Yevtushenko and Enrique Pineda Barnet. Through a series of lush black and white vignettes, the film tells the story of pre-Revolutionary Cuba. The voice of the island narrates in poetic verses during the transitions between each scene. The first vignette features good-time Americans gambling, drinking, and smoking fat cigars in a jungle-themed bar filled with a stable of Cuban women at their disposal. One man ends up with a gorgeous brown-skinned woman who reluctantly calls herself "Betty." When Betty's client asks to see how she really lives, she sighs and takes him across town, over open sewers and unpaved roads, to her shack. When her boyfriend, a fruit vendor, drops in the next morning and catches them, the John rushes out, becomes lost in the maze of shanties, and is surrounded by a group of tugging, begging children. The narrator asks, "Why leave now? You wanted to see it; why not see it all?" How highly ironic that this pre-Revolutionary scenario repeated itself in Cuba after the fall of the Soviet Union, formerly their biggest trading partner and subsidizer. But this time, the clients weren't necessarily American but from other parts of the world, bringing pale skin and thawed-out libidos to the sunbaked island.

43 AÑOS
DE VALOR, UNIDA[D]
Y CONFIANZA
EN LA REVOLUCIÓ[N]

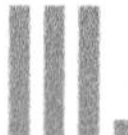

Jake and I called them "our angels in white:" Félix and Abel gliding down Havana's 23rd Street, La Rampa, wearing white shirts and blue jeans on this warm, perfect Caribbean midnight.

At that time in Havana there weren't any gay clubs or bars, whether by official policy or shunned practice. You'd have to hang out on La Rampa or go to the little café on Calle M to find where the *fiesta de diez pesos* would be that night. The location of the parties was spread by word-of-mouth through a vast underground gay network.

The four of us made eye contact and started talking with some clichéd line like "Haven't I seen you before?" After chatting for a moment, we decided to go into a nearby café to spend some time before going out to the party.

We waited inside the ice cream parlor-like place, short on menu offerings but full of cigarette smoke. Félix seemed a little nervous. I had my eye on his friend Abél, with his silky hair, café con leche skin, and stereotypical Latin good looks. Félix was shorter, darker, and somewhat stouter. I learned later that Abél only had eyes for Jake because he was "tired of brown people" and was enchanted by Jake's swimming-pool-blue eyes. While Abél and Jake struggled to communicate in exaggerated (Abél) and broken (Jake) Spanish, Félix and I chatted amicably, but just on the verge of being disinterested. He had a nervous little laugh and kept fanning himself with his hand, complaining about the broken air conditioner, which was turned on but blowing tepid air. Still, it felt better than being outside. Félix wiped his brow and kept chatting, asking me about life in the States and what I did for a living, in which he seemed particularly interested.

Soon, as if charged by noticeable electricity in the hot air, the crowd started to move out of the café and spill onto the sidewalk in front. There was an incredible swirl of men, a mix of bodies in lycra tops or taut solid t-shirts. Men were everywhere, gesturing with expressive hands, flashing bright teeth, and riding the wave of amped up party energy. Abél and Félix negotiated a ride for us with one of the unofficial cab drivers out front. They had no official cab licenses, but they were folks "in the know" with cars and the need for cash. The four of us crammed into a souped-up red subcompact, where the driver was blasting Madonna remixes and chatting with Abél and Félix. My comprehension wasn't nearly good enough to fully catch their conversation, spoken at warp speed and missing half the consonants at the end of words.

We rocketed off through the still streets of Havana, passing landmarks our angels pointed out as we whizzed by. "There's the Plaza de la Revolución and the famous mural of Ché Guevara. There's the Stadio and the Ministry of Communication..."

We headed in the direction of the airport, 25 kilometers outside of town, so I figured that we were going to be in a somewhat remote area. I could see my mother's face at that moment asking, "What are you doing in a speeding car in a foreign land – one with a dictator at that – with people you just met, going to some party out in the middle of the country?" But somehow, I knew we were going to be alright.

Félix, who was sitting in the front seat, reached back to knead my leg, which was jammed up against his back. I was a little surprised at the gesture because he'd been friendly to me, but not that friendly. *Good*, I thought, *maybe this evening would be interesting after all.*

After leaving the main highway we drove through the woods, down a dirt road, over a one-way bridge, through a mango grove, and pulled up to a clearing with a glut of parked cars next to what looked like an unfinished house. The bass-driven pulse of Latin techno music throbbed in the night air. Abél and Félix asked Jake and me for five dollars to pay the cab driver, which we did, and then the four of us proceeded to the front door of the party, where Jake and I peeled off a few more greenbacks for the cover charge. In this social norm it was common for tourists to pay the cover charge to these parties if they're accompanied by locals - like a party-finder's fee.

There in the middle of the forest, the venue looked like some sort of grand Spanish vacation villa never completed by the owners. The outside walls were made of stone and shaped with arches and ledges. Looking up, the night sky shimmered above us. Men mingled on each side of the crowded dance floor in front of the bar and bathrooms in the back.

We jumped into the crowd; Félix gripped my hand tightly as he led me through a spicy salsa/house mix, bringing our faces close enough to feel the sweat steaming off of each other's skin. He twirled me around and around to the crazy loud dance mix. A little dizzy, I grabbed him for balance and we stumbled together, clutching one another to make sure we didn't crash to the ground, which brought us even closer together.

We had our first kiss there on the dance floor, like a scene right out of a romantic comedy; there under the starry sky, holding onto one another while others carried on with party-like-it's-1999 enthusiasm. The men surrounding us added to the lusty and passionate air – men of all shades of brown from chestnut/mahogany to pale beige, reflecting the nation's indigenous, African, and European heritages all rolled into one grinding, sweating, chatting mass. Throughout the night, Jake and I kept looking at each other with disbelief – was this really happening to us?

Of course, I kept remembering *Soy Cuba*, and was uncomfortable with the possibility of coming off like a new-day colonizer, bringing in money (the little bit that I had), having my way with the "natives," whooping it up and then flying out. But even that PC guilt didn't keep me from enjoying the company and caresses of this handsome man.

Several times during the night Félix asked me for money for drinks, money for rum, money for Cokes, money to buy his friends Cokes and rum and drinks. He was courteous, though. At least he'd proceed his requests with "*¿Quieres algo?*" – Do you want anything? – before asking for five dollars. No, this definitely wasn't a cheap date. I noticed, though, that Jake wasn't having to shell out cash to Abél, who seemed content with struggling through their stuttered conversations and smooching my friend with great enthusiasm.

Félix was a great kisser. His mouth tasted slightly sweet from the rum and Coke, and he used just the right combination of tongue, lip, nibble, suck, and pressure to keep my rapt attention.

So here Jake and I were, in the middle of a forest with Latin house music as the soundtrack for the night, drenched in sweat, and delighting in the chance to make out madly with these two delicious Habañeros, our angels.

Dizzy with lust but completely worn out by 3 a.m., we decided to return to our hotel. The same guy who gave us a ride out to the party was parked in front waiting for us in the little souped-up red subcompact. Jake and I arranged to meet with Abél and Félix at 8 p.m. the next day for a real double date, with dinner and entertainment afterwards. As we pulled up in front of the hotel where Jake and I were staying, I took out money to pay the driver and somebody's hand pushed mine closer to the floor, out of eye level of anybody who may have been looking into the car from outside.

"¡Shh! ¡La policía!"

I didn't see any police around, but nevertheless I slipped the cash to Félix, who then asked me for $8 or $9 so that he could get a cab ride back to his house. He said that he lived too far from the hotel to walk, and didn't have money for a cab ride. I begrudgingly handed a few extra bucks to him, again noticing that Abél was going to make his way home without asking Jake for any assistance. I later found out that it only costs $3 to get from the hotel to Félix's house.

The next morning (four hours later to be exact), our hotel room phone rang, jarring me out of a ragged sleep. The receptionist said I had a guest named Félix waiting for me in the lobby. I was shocked that he was there at that hour. Of course he couldn't come right up to our room because at the time, local citizens, unless they were working in a hotel or otherwise had special permission, weren't allowed in tourists' rooms. Allegedly Castro sought to eliminate the (booming) sex trade by cutting down on the number of places where people could rendezvous, hotel rooms being the obvious target. So Félix stayed in the lobby while I prepared to come down. Even that was risky for Félix – interacting with a tourist could bring a fine or worse from the police.

I dragged myself up feeling like Lazarus rising, threw on some clothes, and stumbled downstairs, still smelly and groggy from the late night and lingering jet lag. Félix greeted me with a serious face. "Can we talk?"

"Sure." I was certain he wasn't going to announce that he was pregnant or that I'd given him an STD, so I wondered what the too-early morning call was about. He led me to a point just off the hotel's grounds where he would be more comfortable sitting and chatting, away from the ever-present eyes of hotel security.

"Why are you here?" I asked him. "We're supposed to get together tonight, not this morning."

"I just wanted to have a chance to talk with you."

"About what?"

"Things are really hard right now for my family. My mother has no job, my stepfather works at night, and we're taking care of my sister and nephew. All of us are living in a little apartment." He'd already told me the previous night of how he didn't have a job and was finishing up the equivalent of a trade degree. I wondered if he was too dark and too poor to land a job in the hotel industry. So between the five of them in his family, only one person had an actual, regular source of income.

He didn't directly ask for money. "Anything you can do to help will be appreciated. Anything you can do."

"Well, we'll see about all that." Not wanting to be an exploiter, I felt a certain sense of duty to help out. But at that moment, with crusty eyes, pre-caffeine cloudiness, and morning breath, I wasn't prepared to do anything. Before parting ways, we agreed to meet later that night, as we'd originally agreed, at 8 p.m. in front of the hotel. I went right back upstairs and went to sleep, though a little troubled.

That evening, Abél and Félix met us right on time in front of the hotel, immaculately dressed, waiting for us to arrive. In fact, they were early, contrary to any Latin American reputation for tardiness. They had decided to take us to a nearby *paladar*, one of the private restaurants run by individual citizens largely outside the oversight of the State. Evidently Abél knew one of the owners, and by bringing us there, he could get a small commission. But of course, I found out about that later.

We hailed a cab to take us to the paladar. Just like the previous night, it wasn't an official cab, but some guy with a cigar who looked like he could use the extra Washingtons while out for a ride with his girlfriend (his wife was at home). From 1993 to 2004, the U.S. dollar was legal tender in Cuba – a delicious irony that Yanqui money directly helped to boost Socialismo. One Yanqui dollar was roughly equal to 20 Cuban pesos, the currency most Cubans are paid in and deal with on a daily basis. Because of the dual currencies, two social classes began to emerge: one with access to dollars and one without. The folks who have access to dollars usually work in the tourism industry in some capacity, and access to these jobs are highly regulated by the government. I noticed that the majority of people connected to tourism were white or light-skinned. Those without access to dollars, or the "poorer" people I saw in Centro Habana, were as dark or darker than I am. Unmistakably black. So a regular José with a working car – like this driver – had little side-gigs in order to get paid in dollars, which could earn him the equivalent of a month's pay in a single night. And this was way before Uber.

We set out for the paladar – the driver and his girlfriend in the front seat; and Abél, Jake, Félix, and me in the back. Thin notes from an acoustic guitar drifted from the radio while we glided through town in one of the classic old sedans from the 1950s miraculously kept in working order long after most of their U.S. counterparts had been sold for scrap parts. Whenever the car was in motion, Félix and I explored each other's tongues and lips while a light breeze whispered through the car window. His passion, his kiss, and the general romantic ambience of the evening drove me mad with desire. I didn't want to get too worked up, since we couldn't go anywhere to take it to the next level, and I didn't want to be walking from the car with a big wet bulge in my khakis.

Damn, I wanted him! I was starving for physical affection, and being on the receiving end of his touch didn't help me forget my months-old celibacy. We hadn't yet figured out where we could go to be alone though, since he lived with four other people, and he couldn't come up to my hotel room. There was nothing to do but hold back.

Once seated in the paladar, the four of us joked around and compared observations on life in Havana and California. The food was good and the portions were big. Jake didn't eat much because he was still full from our earlier lunch, but not only did Félix devour his own food, he finished off Jake's pork and had a big helping of arroz con pollo as well. He downed two beers and still looked around like he was ready to consume more.

"What an appetite! Are you pregnant?" I said, referring to Félix's little belly and enormous appetite.

"Noo, soy macho," he said – recoiling at the thought of being compared to a woman, even jokingly. He was straight up macho, all man, and one with a big appetite. I made some sort of light

comment as penance so he would stop pouting, even though his paunch and ravenous appetite did make him look like he was expecting a child in five months.

The next night, we sat on the Malecón staring out into the dark surf and sky. Jake and I were set to leave Havana the next day and head to Varadero, a resort community exclusively for foreigners. That plan sounded good when we first made up our itinerary, but now I regretted having to leave Havana and my sweet, handsome, hungry loverman so early in the game.

"I'm having a good time. I wish I could spend more time with you before I have to leave," I told Félix.

"I do too. I want to keep in touch with you. *Eres muy cariñoso* – you are very caring. And I appreciate you wanting to help me and my family. There's no hope here. I want to leave this place. There are no jobs for people like me. Unless you're a good party member, you end up working for almost nothing. I want...freedom." He said the word quietly and looked around, wanting to make sure he wasn't in earshot of anyone but me. No one could be trusted with that word in this place where the walls have eyes and ears.

My lowered tone matched Félix's. "You wouldn't ever get on a boat, would you?" I asked, recalling stories of Cubans landing on Florida shores – all skin and bones – after a treacherous trip across the sea.

"No, no, no. That's too dangerous. I would never do that. I know of possible ways that are safer. I just need some help."

"Well, maybe I can. You have to tell me what to do, though, because I have no idea."

"In the meantime, you can help by going to the dollar store and buying my family some basic things. My mother needs some good lotion for her hands. They're dried out from always washing clothes. We also need some soap. I could also use some new clothes."

"I don't know if I can help with the clothes right now," I said, even though I would've given him the shirt off of my back, "but maybe tomorrow I can get the other things for you. Can we meet tomorrow?"

We agreed on a time and place, at a hotel café near his home in Centro Habana. In the shadows of a small cluster of trees, we shared a final kiss, which would be our last one for six months.

Early the next morning I sat straight up in the bed. My usual grogginess was replaced by adrenaline-fueled clarity; I had a mission on my mind. We were scheduled to leave Havana at noon, so I had to take care of business quickly. Many of the items which are in scarce supply in the peso economy – just about everything – were available in the dollar stores, where U.S. greenbacks were king. Our hotel, a tourist-only destination, had such a store. I went to the gift shop and bought lotion, deodorant, aspirin, soap, and pens. I got envelopes and paper. I bought a nice shirt and put everything in a cheap backpack so that the handoff to Félix would look more inconspicuous. This was as close to international intrigue as I was going to get – buying contraband for my lover of three days and slyly handing it off in a smoky café before walking away without an emotional goodbye.

We were set to meet in the café of a small but well-known hotel near his apartment in Centro Habana. Félix showed up a few minutes late, the first time he had been late to meet me, wearing shades and a pout, which I would later come to see as his normal "street face." The first three buttons on his bright royal blue shirt were open, enough so I could see the kinky curls on his cocoa chest. God, I wanted to kiss him so badly. He was even more gorgeous than I'd remembered. Or maybe he appeared so because I was leaving in a few hours and thought it quite possible that we would never meet again.

We entered the café and sat without much fanfare or affection. I was sad. Here was an *hombre* who kissed me wet and open and hungrily. Who paid attention to attention-starved me. Who made me feel wanted and useful and attractive. I wanted more. At that moment, though, I couldn't read what he was thinking. He seemed a little withdrawn, a little nervous. I didn't know whether I was making him uncomfortable, but then he asked to order a sandwich.

"I put a few things in the bag that I think might be useful for you. I even have pens and paper so that you can write me in the States." The backpack was on a chair at the table.

"*Grácias.* I'll be sure to write. You'll get a surprise around your birthday." That date was three weeks away.

"I look forward to it. Keep your faith. Something good will happen, and I'm going to try to be helpful."

As we were leaving, he picked up the backpack and slung it over one shoulder. He had me leave first and walk in front of him until we crossed the street, so that hotel security wouldn't see us leaving together since we'd arrived separately. We walked to a taxi queue nearby. Félix wished me a safe journey and implored me to keep in touch. "I will never forget you," he said.

"I won't forget you either. And remember my birthday," I half-joked.

He cracked a tiny smile. "I will."

"Be careful." I got into one of the cabs and he shut the door. As we drove away, I watched as his blue shirt grew smaller and smaller in the distance. How frustrating was the stilted goodbye, the fact that we couldn't kiss there in public, the lack of time and freedom to get to know each other better, his living within the confines of a police state, and an economic embargo that keeps him and so many of his countrymen living on the edge, with just enough to stay alive but little else.

After the encounters with Felix, Varadero was a superficial Caribbean Disneyworld. There were sumptuous buffets at mealtime and cornucopia-wearing tropical caricatures at showtime painting a vivid, happy picture of the island. Even the colors seemed brighter here, not faded by the day-to-day grind. Jake and I both felt guilty knowing that we had access to this food, these resort facilities, and this stunning beach while our Habanero angels, would be barred from it all. Whoever said politics make sense?

***

For some reason people always expect to tell and hear post-vacation travel stories of sun, sand, sea, and sex. My return to the States was no exception - everybody wanted juicy details, and I didn't disappoint (even though I had no sex tales to tell).

I was enchanted. I couldn't forget Félix. I charmed my friends with his handsome photo and turned them on with descriptions of rum-sweetened tropical passion. But my friends were also realists, some of them wondering aloud how we'd make anything work across a distance and language barrier, not to mention a 40-year-old embargo. Of course I dismissed their concerns with a faith that people are bigger than rules and that love is bigger than governments. Aren't they? Never mind that I wasn't quite in love, only having interacted with this man for a little over three days. I'd never felt this feeling before and had it returned. I've known the rollercoaster climb and crash of unrequited love, and this wasn't the same vibe as that. I didn't have the same sense of desperation. Or did I? Part of me felt desperate to get him out of Cuba. I felt desperate to get him to the States to be with me. I was tired of being alone, which is strange, given that I lived in what was once both the epicenter and the cutting edge of the gay universe: San Francisco. A plain-looking, decent-bodied, somewhat introverted, somewhat sensitive man like me didn't stand a chance in this scene. Dating rarely happened for me, if it happened at all. Blackness is not popular here, and black men are still second-class erotic citizens, being neither exotic enough, next-door enough, or in the eyes of some, trustworthy enough.

At the same time, I seemed to have limited appeal to other black gay men, many living across the Bay in Oakland, a 15 minute drive that sometimes seems worlds apart. To those men, the fact that I lived in San Francisco was an indictment of bad racial politics: "you live in The City so you *must* be exclusively into white men," they'd sniff and accuse, looking down noses over razor-thin goatees. However untrue that was (I like all flavors), I was too psyched out by my own plainness and lack of game to make much progress.

To add insult to injury, the last guy I briefly dated told me that I wasn't masculine enough for him. I'm not sure what standard of masculinity I needed to meet, but I just wasn't masculine "enough." Félix had none of those worries - color, masculinity, or charisma...at least none that he told me about during our time together. So it had come to this, my shot at love. This was why I had to be open to all options, including a foreign one. And no one dared tell me to drop it. They admired my idealism and kept their questions about my rationalizing and justifying to themselves. At least I think they did.

"Plus," my tell-it-like-it-is friend Ben said, looking me up and down in the all-knowing way that only older black queens can tell all your business, "I knew that you needed something imported. This little domestic stuff here won't work for you, chile."

Félix and I relied on emails and the occasional letter, expensive to send and slow to arrive, to convey our heat and hope. Before the widespread use of social media for constant and near instant contact, email was a saving grace for two people trying to find love over the miles and beyond an embargo.

I especially loved the many nicknames; every positive, beautiful, affectionate title he could think of. *Mi oceano. Mi tesoro. Mi amorcito. Mi fresa y chocolate. Mi sol. Mi cielo.* He made me swoon like a reclusive great aunt holding a velvet-lined treasure box full of secret memories. Only my good times weren't going to be limited to memories. I was going to have my cake and eat him too.

IV.

UNO

Cuidad Habana
El Año de Nuestro Encuentro, Unión, y Amistad
Year of Our Meeting, Union, and Friendship

¡Hola mi amor! ¿Todo bien?

Mi amor querido, I wish that these little letters find you well in health and happy with your family and friends. *Mi fresa y chocolate,* I'll tell you that I feel nostalgic since you left. With you gone, I miss having someone to talk with and appreciate. Since you arrived in my heart with the way that you kissed me with your sweet mouth, I am filled with much positive energy. Every day now I am in my house looking at photos of us together during the days that passed when we were getting to know each other, and the happy moments that we shared side by side. I wish, *mi amor,* that some day we will return to the place of knowing each other again and spending time together again, and I promise you that you'll be the happiest man in the world. I will give you all of the love and calor that you need. I'll kiss every inch of your body and leave you listless. *Mi amorcito,* thinking about these things makes my desire grow strong.

I will also tell you that at this moment I am studying English from the book you sent me. I am very thankful to you for this book because you want and wish the best for me, and for this I adore you and I need you at my side to give you all of the *calor* you need. I promise you that someday we will be together again. But *mi amor,* we have to have lots of patience so that these things can come soon and safely. I ask God every morning to take care of you and to send you much positive energy, the same energy that you have waiting for you here in Cuba. Your *gran Cubanito* prays so that you will continue being well wherever you are. Never feel insecure, always remember that on a small and humble island there is a *gran* prince who is waiting for his princess (joke). *Te adoro.*

DOS

Mi querido y estimado amor, I hope that these words of love and caring find you healthy and happy.

Mi amor, I am very happy in knowing that you always have me in your thoughts and in your heart, just as I have you in mine. My dear mother and sister are very happy with the photograph of you, and feel like they know you already, but of course they want to know you in person some day. *Mi amor,* I feel a great nostalgia for you and I want to be near you RIGHT NOW to give you all of the love and caring that I feel for you.

I am sure that being side by side we would be the happiest duo in the world. It is strange that I feel that I have known you for a long time, but something has awakened in me that I haven't ever felt, and never this strongly before.

Mi amor, how the memory of your kisses drives me crazy, your warm hugs and your sweet and passionate way of looking at me – how all of these things still bring your memory to my eyes.

My family, *Gracias a Dios,* is well and sends you greetings. I like that you have told your family about me. Now you will have a new member for Christmas festivities!

I am loving you and needing you little by little. Take care of yourself and love me a lot. Don't get with anyone else, ok, since I am CUBAN and I'm jealous! I looooooooove you and I want yoooooooooooou in my life.

Can you imagine what would happen if I were there with you, what I would do with you, this crazy Cuban that you have on your hands? I will love you like no one has ever done before, I will take you to a place in love where you have never been. I will kidnap you with my caresses until they carry you to that same moon that you saw the other night and thought of me. I will fill you with kisses and I will make you feel inside who this *gran Cubano* is. IMAGINE.

Writing this has made me a little nervous and agitated...horny!... I want to feel you RIGHT NOW!

Mi vida, take care of yourself and please return soon here. *Bueno mi amor,* I say goodbye caringly, and send greetings from *tu Cubanito* that loves you and won't forget you. A big kiss on all the places where I didn't give you any before.

Chao.
Félix

TRÉS

Hola querido amor. I hope that you are well in all areas of your life.

I have many wishes to see you. I hope that we can meet again soon and that the distance won't be an obstacle for our love. I miss you a lot and hope that you also miss me and are thinking about me in all of the moments that I am here waiting for your return.

I wish I could buy you the CD you asked for but here they are very expensive and I don't have money for it.

Remember that I love you and you are always in my thoughts.

About the phone card: here it is impossible to use it since we don't have the technology for it. This is why I haven't called you. Plus, I don't have a phone, remember.

Te quiero mucho, tu Cubanito
Félix

CUATRO

Hola. I hope you are well in all aspects of your life.

I am very happy from your mail and the beautiful things that you tell me. I want you to know that I also dream of you and the days that pass, thinking of you and the marvelous and unforgettable moments that we spent together.

Right now I am sad since my grandfather passed away this past Tuesday. I am pained by his death, but that's how life is and we have to live through these things.

I hope that you will write me soon and tell me of your work and your things, when you feel tired thinking of me.

I want to ask you a favor and hope that you don't take this badly. *Mi amorcito,* you were able to appreciate the conditions that you saw when you were here in Cuba, and the great needs that we Cubans have. I want to see if you can, within your possibilities, send me $100 so that I can buy shoes and clothes and have a dinner in my home for my birthday, which we will hold in honor of you. I want to make a dinner for my mother, sister, and a few friends – the ones that you met and who always ask me about you. I also want to buy different kinds of medicine that is available at the dollar store. With the peso, there is nothing but sadness – you can't buy anything with the peso, especially medicine. But don't become sad, *mi amor*, my mother and sister and I will be very thankful for the help that you are going to provide.

Mi amorcito, please don't be upset by my request because I need your help in this moment, and I don't like asking for it since I really only want to love you and to be loved. *Mi cielo,* if you are going to send the money, please tell me (through email) the number that the *Werter Yonio* people give to you so that I'll be able to get the money here in Cuba without a problem.

If you can, please send the money before my birthday, because I want to be able to buy shoes and clothes and food for the dinner and food for our house. Please don't forget to send the number! I will always be thankful to you. I only wish the best for you and want to be at your side. I'm not a timid person, but very observant and I like to love and make love to you, because you deserve it, my love.

Mi oceano, I'm going to try to send a few gifts to you, and I hope they will make you very happy because I want you to be happy. *Mi amor,* I will not leave you but will only say goodbye until that next time we meet. Please write soon. *Saludos* to your good friend in San Francisco who was with you here in Cuba (I forgot his name) and a million kisses for you on your beautiful mouth.

CINCO

Mi querido amor, every day I grow happier and more content with our friendship of love and hope that you are well and happy. You have met a great love who knows how to value the sentiments of love and for this reason, *mi amor*, I want to give to you a million kisses to celebrate one month of knowing you. Perhaps you thought that I forgot this date, but *amor*, forgive me if I didn't send congratulations and all of those marvelous things. I want to say that I don't want to finish this letter. This is part of the love that I feel for you.

Mi amor, I received your messages and am very thankful to you for sending the little gift through la *Werter Yonio. Mi amorcito*, take care. Your *gran Cubanito* loves you and won't forget you. Don't forget your jealous *lobo*. I won't say farewell but goodbye and until the next time. A million kisses on your body and in your beautiful mouth, *mi gran amor*.

Tu macho,
Félix

SEIS

Mi queridísimo amor, it is my strongest wishes that you are happy and healthy with your friends and family. *Mi amor*, I received your message that you sent me the money and I am very thankful for your generosity. I am very proud to be part of you, *mi tesoro*. I think of you all of the time and I know that you also think of me too, and I need your company. *Te amo* and I don't want to stop thinking of you. Since you're not here, I hope you'll carry me in your heart and thoughts. *Mi amor*, tomorrow I will go to *la Werter Yonio* to pick up the money and Saturday I will tell you how much I have received. *Bueno, mi amor,* take care and know that here very far away there is a prince who loves you much!

Tu Cubanito,
Félix

SIETE

Mi querido amor. May the receipt of this letter find you happy and healthy along with your friends and companions. *Mi fresa y chocolate,* I am very thankful for your generosity for the grand favor that you are doing for me and my family. My dear mother and my sister wish you much happiness and good health and luck and that you take care of yourself. Here we only speak of you and how your family are doing after the tragic events in America. *Bueno, mi amorcito,* I received the money that you sent to me through *Werter Yonio. Grácias, mi amor,* now tomorrow morning I will go get the second payment with the number that you sent me.

Mi tesoro, I am very happy to know that you have made plans to return to Cuba in January to study at the University. I wish it were in October, *mi amor,* but I know that that is impossible since you have to work to be able to visit me and be at my side. You will improve your Spanish and help with my English and we will have a grand time together. *Mi amor,* when you come to Cuba, don't reserve a hotel since here we have *casas particulares* that you can rent and I will be able to be with you all of the time. We are a pair, *una pareja,* and it doesn't matter to me what other people will say since there are always people who don't agree. *Mi cariño, te deseo* and I always think of you wherever I am. I tell you, *mi amor,* that we should always trust each other so that things will be a little bit better for us. *Bueno, mi amor,* I don't want to close this letter and thoughts of you but I must leave this moment as time is passing. I love you and will not forget you. I am very happy that you are coming back.

Until the next letter, take care from your *Cubanito* that loves you always – Felicito (What a wonderful name – this is what we will call our children – joke!). *Chao.*

OCHO

Hola mi amorcito, I got all of your messages and am very happy and thankful to you. I am always thinking of you. Here in Cuba we talk a lot about you and I hope that time is on our side and will bring you back so I can give you all of the *calor* that you deserve. I am here waiting with much patience and thinking about the day that you return to Cuba and how it will be a marvelous one. My dear mother sends you greetings for health and happiness along with your family and friends. When you are here in Cuba, *amor,* we will make a dinner and invite my mother. What do you think?

Mi amor, how great that a friend is coming to Cuba; I will give him a letter for you and a few gifts so that you will remember me, too. I don't only want to have memories of you, I want you to have memories of me, too, ok, because that will make me jealous (joke)! *Mi fresa y chocolate, mi cariño,* I want to ask you if it is within your possibilities to send with your friend who is coming to Cuba a little bit of money so that I can eat and buy my mother a washer since she has bad hands and can't wash. *Amor,* I have the money that you sent the last time but I haven't used it. I am saving it and only have to get $200 because I have $100. Don't take this badly, ok, my mother will be very thankful to you. If you can't send all of the money to me with your friend it's okay, you can send it little by little. You are a great love, a great friend, for understanding all of these things. Don't worry about buying me any clothes. You can bring these things when you come visit me. *Bueno, mi amorcito,* I don't want to close this letter but the hours are passing and the phone card [for email] is running out. I won't forget you and I love you very much. Until the next letter, *te amo mi tesoro*, send me the address where I can go pick up the packet from your friend. *Chao, te quiero.*

NUEVE

Hola mi dulce chocolate, how are you? I'm glad to be in this new conversation with you across the miles. *Mi amorcito*, I feel very happy and thankful for your gifts that you sent for me with much love and caring, and for this I feel a strong desire to see you to give you all of my love. *Mi cielo*, you are a person of great significance to me. God wanted us to be together. *Mi freso*, yesterday when I finished sending the message to you I went to the hotel where your *compañero* is staying and presented myself to him, a very respectable man. Thank you for everything and I will send with him the photographs of my family and my friends so that you can know who they are and when you are here in Cuba, you will know them personally and we will have a wedding party and a dinner with them (what do you think, *mi amor?*). *Mi querer*, my dear mother is very happy with the gifts that you have sent her and my sister is very thankful and happy and they want to have a dinner with us when you arrive. *Amor*, thanks for sending the picture of you and your friends on your birthday. I'm very proud of it and happy to know you. I also received the money that you sent for me, which I will use to buy things for myself and my home. *Bueno, mi amor*, I won't say farewell to you, I'll only say *adiós* and until the next letter (which I'll send with your *compañero*). Okay, *cuidate mucho* and behave.

Tu hombre Cubano, Félix.

I'll send you gifts so you'll remember me, too. *Te quiero, te amo, te necesito.*

DIEZ

Hola mi amor, I hope that when you receive this letter you will be full of health and happiness with your family and friends. *Mi amor,* I am very unhappy because you can't get the photographs and the gifts from me. I went to the hotel on Sunday early in the morning and the woman at the hotel told me that your *compañero* had left already on Saturday. *Amor,* I was carrying the camera and a few gifts for you and your *compañero* (I took photos of me and my family). Saturday night we had a party for the *santo* of my mother and paid homage to him and others were at the party, particularly my friends that met you when you were in Cuba. *Mi tesoro,* I wanted to send you the letters and the gifts, but that's not important *mi amor;* the important thing is that I love you and want the best for you. Although we are too far from each other I am always thinking of you. My dear mother sends you greetings and hopes that you are well and happy with your friends. *Mi amor,* I'm going to develop the photos here in Cuba and wait for a friend of yours to come to Cuba so that I can send them to you like you asked. *Mi amor,* always remember that on this island there is a great love who thinks of you every day.

Mi amor, please explain to your *compañero* everything that happened so that he won't consider me a man of no learning and no manners. *Bueno, mi amor,* I won't say farewell to you, only goodbye until the next letter. Oh, *mi querido,* don't reserve a hotel since I made a reservation for you in a *casa particular* in Vedado, one that is very close to the *paladar* where we ate with our friends. *Mi amor,* if you prefer I can send you the letter that I wanted to send with your *compañero* through the regular mail. *Bueno, mi amor,* I don't want to close this letter but I must. Ok, we will see each other soon, your Félix, your *Cubanito,* a million kissssssesssssssssss. I adore you and can't forget you and soon you will be by my side. *Chao.*

ONCE

Hola mi amor. All is good. *Bueno mi cariño*, I got your messages and I know that you are very anxious to see the photos. Here everything is good. *Mi tesoro*, I am very happy to know that you are looking forward to being in *mi Habana*, so that we can be together and spend moments of happiness together, the two of us. When you are a guest at the *casa particular* you can come with another friend so that the rent is cheaper and you won't have to stay in a hotel and this way we can be together the two weeks that you're going to be here. Don't leave me alone by staying in a hotel, *mi amor*, please talk to another friend and this way things will be better for all of us (*amor*, what do you think?). In any case, we have a month before we have to decide what to do. *Bueno*, as soon as the photos arrive, *mi amor*, I will send them to you without a problem and I am sincere that I don't have any money, if you could send me some so that I can send you the photos with all of my positive energy. *Bueno mi amor*, until the next letter, I hope that you are very happy with your friends from work. *Mi amor* I send greetings to your family and hope that they are well. *Bueno mi tesoro*, all that is left for me to say is that I will always adore you. *Chao.*

DOCE

Hola mi amor, I am well, but it wasn't easy with the hurricane. I couldn't communicate with you since we didn't have electricity. *Mi cielo*, thank God that we are recuperating because our city and Cuba were very affected but we are coming back. *Mi amor*, my family is well, and we send you many thanks because you were worried about us. *Mi cielo*, I am very thankful for the money that you sent me since it will help us a lot now that we need food for the house and with the hurricane we didn't have enough food and it was a great trial. My love, many thanks for your generosity. *Bueno mi amor*, as always I am very anxious because you are going to be here in Cuba at my side.

Mi cielo you told me that you will be in the hotel for one week to save money and one week in the *casa particular. Mi amor*, if that is what you want then that is what we will do. Or you could be by my side for 15 days in a *casa particular*. You decide since I will be waiting, okay.

TRECE

Hola mi amor, todo bien. Each day I am thankful for you since you are concerned about my family. *Mi querer*, today I send you another letter in the mail. *Mi cielo*, I know that letters take a long time to get to you, but the important thing is that we don't lose our communication. *Mi amor*, now I have a problem. I don't have phone cards to communicate through email, I will have to send you an email every two weeks since we don't have regular email service. The hurricane affected the electricity and the communications. Okay *mi amor*, don't be mad because this will only last a little while. *Mi amor*, don't worry because I will write and send a letter through the mail. Okay *mi amor*, when you send the money please put the address of my house since the last time that you send money through *Werter Yonio* you put my post office box address. Don't worry *mi amor* I got the money, but remember to put my home address. Okay *mi amor*, I will write you on Friday when you send the money. Okay.

CATORCE

Hola mi amor, todo bien. I got your message and am writing you because a friend loaned me a few of his minutes so that I could communicate with you. I also sent you two certified letters that will probably take a while but you will be certain to get them. Okay. We're still having problems with the email after the hurricane. Oh I am very happy that you made pumpkin soup and want you to make some for me when we are together. *Amor*, when we are together we will go to Trinidad de Cuba as you wish.

My pants size is 32 and shoes are 42 and shirt is a small.

When you send money put my home address. When phone cards are available I will write you.

A kiss,
Félix

QUINCE

Hola mi querido. Every day I am happy because our encounter has almost arrived and I want to hug you and embrace you and have you very close to me to give you all of the *calor* that you need because you are the person for me that I appreciate and love and for this *mi cielo*, I need you by my side. *Mi querer*, I understand you today that you will be in the hotel for several days and other days with your true love because I need you and you need me. *Mi amor* you also should bring with you your driver's license so that we can go to the beach and to other tourist places here in La Habana like Soroa and Viñales and discos to dance salsa and spend moments of happiness together. *Bueno mi amor*, I love you and will be together with you very soon. I always have you on my mind. Be sure to tell me the day and the hour that you will arrive in Cuba so that I can wait at your hotel.

V.

I was glad to be off the plane after a seven-hour flight. When I was a kid, I'd hear what seemed like regular reports on the evening news about hijackers taking over planes and flying them to Cuba. Presumably the hijackers were let go and allowed to live free. Twenty years later, I wonder if the former hijackers still consider themselves to be free, after their reputations had melted away, a new generation of policía had taken over the neighborhood patrols, and the day-to-day scruffiness of life had found its way underneath their nails.

Félix last wrote that he would meet me at the hotel. But rather than being excited en route, I had cold feet. I sat in a dark cab wondering what I was doing and whether I should even be there, spending more time and money on this most complex of long distance relationships. I wondered whether Félix really cared about me, and deep down, whether I was mistaking love for what was actually neediness, for being able to say "I have a boyfriend."

The taxi wound through the wind-swept, nearly deserted Havana streets. I was pleased to recognize certain landmarks from my previous visit: the Plaza de la Revolución, where the famous Ché Guevara mural loomed large, peered sternly out over the massive square. We passed the Universidad de la Habana, where I would be studying during my two-week stay in Havana, giving me a legal reason to travel to Cuba. The University sits grand atop a hill looking out on double-laned streets winding down into the pleasant residential neighborhood of Vedado. One of the most memorable scenes in the movie *Soy Cuba* is of a student rally and protest there at the steps of the University: the streets are filled with students, who begin a peaceful and defiant march. The leader of the march holds over his head a slain dove, shot by the guardians of the old regime, while other students fall in to march behind him. In short order they're met by the chaotic and brutal full force of dictator Batista's henchmen, armed with fire hoses, nightsticks, tear gas, and bullets. But that night in front of the University, the reenacted protest was just a wispy memory alongside me and the cabdriver.

I recognized the Habana Libre Hotel and the Hotel Nacionál, anchoring their respective places in the Havana skyline. I remembered the Malecón, lining the northern shore of the city. After finding out that I am from the U.S. and not Jamaica, the cab driver remarked, "Figure out how to build a 90-mile bridge from the Malecón to Florida, and Cuba would empty out overnight."

We pulled up to the hotel, located right on the Malecón. It was kind of 1980s modern, blocks and stone with a small polished inside lobby, nothing ornate or evoking throwback memories of casinos and cigars. Its nondescript efficient look could have put it anywhere in the world. The registration clerk, looking like a brunette fashion model, told me that a *"muchacho"* had been by to see me, but she'd mistakenly told him that I would arrive the following day, so he'd left. No tip for her!

I lugged my stuff up to the room, as plain and clean as a sparsely-furnished college dorm room – linoleum floors, an overhead light and no lamps, three beds, and a small bathroom. After I'd bumbled around for a few minutes, the phone rang. Félix was calling from the lobby. Adrenaline shot through me. His voice was deeper than I'd remembered, and smooth like a mellow rum, making me feel warm and comfortable. Caught in the moment and out of practice, I suddenly couldn't piece together enough Spanish to speak coherently. Fortunately, Félix took charge, saying that he'd wait for me in the lobby for a few minutes while I prepared to come downstairs.

He was more gorgeous than I remembered. His skin was smoother
and more cocoa-brown than I remembered. He was more youthful than I remembered. He was more serene than I remembered,
and definitely more trim. His lips, which I'd sampled so extensive-
ly and missed so intensely, were slightly puckered and plump. My
heart jumped when I saw him.

Our embrace was a little stifled, given that someone is always
watching, and encounters in hotels are especially suspect. Félix
regarded me in the way that he always looked at me, pleased, with
just barely a hint of a smile tugging up the side of his mouth. He
spoke most openly with his eyes: I loved looking into them, deep
chestnut brown with long eyelashes. They were shaped like he
was sleepy and had just awakened. His skin was flawless, without marks and nicks from shaving or a junk food diet. His hair,
jet black and wavy, would be considered "good" by the folks back
home. He even once referred to his hair being straighter because
of some distant Italian ancestor, something he seemed to speak
of with pride. I wasn't impressed, since so many New World Africans are a genetic blend of African, European, and Indian blood.
Plus, I'm happy to be nappy, as the saying goes.

Leaving the hotel, we tried to go up to the *paladar* where we'd
eaten months earlier, but it was closed. Félix led me to another
place on the third floor of a rather plain steel and tile apartment
building. While climbing the deserted staircase, he turned and
pressed me against the wall for a deep, "I've missed you" kiss. It
wasn't a long one, but the message came across loud and clear.
At that moment, I had no doubt that he had real feelings because
passion like that couldn't be faked. I certainly was happy to taste
his mouth again, slightly sweet like a berry.

The apartment *paladar* smelled of an unsavory combination of burnt oil and cigarette smoke. The owners had taken pride with the setting, and decorated the tables with carefully-arranged linen and handmade napkins with a red and yellow pattern. The window trimmings matched the napkins and linen. Plastic flowers sat in little vases on each table, and although the walls were worn and somewhat stained, the place was quite neat.

Generally, these *paladares* serve chicken, pork, and fish. Steak, lobster, and shellfish are reserved for the state-owned restaurants. Not being much of a meat eater, I became accustomed to ordering the fish and counting on Félix's enormous appetite to finish the rest. Sure enough, he did. That particular evening, he had pork and I had the fish, a flaky hot filet smothered in onions and a lemony sauce. As with every dinner, a heap of black beans and rice - *congrí* - were piled on the side. I treated myself to *plátanos*, which were tender and golden and almost honey-sweet. The meal was very good, and there was lots of it. Félix finished it all. I thought he would lick the plate. He also ordered two beers and asked for some of my fish, of which I gave him a taste.

After I paid the bill, which was the equivalent of eating in a restaurant at home (no bargain to be had here), we headed over to the café on Calle M where we'd first chatted. There wasn't the same kind of summertime electricity in the air as before. A cold front had moved across the Straits of Florida just as I'd arrived, dropping the temperatures into the upper 50s - brisk for a tropical island. Still, the *locas* were not to be denied a Friday night party. The café was the gathering point for anyone who wanted to find out about that night's fiesta, or who wanted a ride there.

We ran into some of Félix's friends; upon introduction my name sounded unpronounceable, a ridiculous Anglo tongue-twister, so I became the *norteamericano*. It felt like one step short of *"gringo"*

and one-and-a-half from "*yanqui.*" I much preferred "*moreno*" or
"cho-co-la-te," pronouncing every syllable like a Spanish cocoa
delight, but "*el norteamericano*" stuck. Félix was the fixer for the
evening, finding others who were interested in going to the party
and knew of rides. He negotiated a ride for us in an old model
Lada, a tiny, boxy Russian sedan reminiscent of a Yugo. *Just don't
drive crazy,* I thought, *so my mama doesn't have to fly my dead
body back to the States after I was trying to find an all-men's party
with my no-English-speaking Cuban boyfriend.* But I got in the
car anyway.

We took off and headed out of the city center, then into the coun-
tryside outside of Havana. We ended up on what looked like a large
farm, judging from the tool sheds and parked tractors. I handed
a thin wad of cash to Félix so he could handle the payments for
the driver and the cover charge. The party organizers had rigged
the speakers around a small corral, creating an outdoor dirt dance
floor. A storage shed with an open window became the concession
stand, selling beer, Tropicola, and rum. There was a good sized
crowd, about 100 men milling around, dancing a bit, and ani-
matedly talking. We bumped our way into the dance corral and
grooved to a pretty fierce Latin house mix.

Throughout the evening, Félix continued to introduce me to
a number of his friends at the party. I especially hit it off with
Agustín, who reminded me of friends back home. He was very
funny and outgoing in a warm and girly way, with big ears that
stuck out from his head like a handsome human Dumbo the El-
ephant. Around three in the morning, the party started tapering
off. Abél, Diego, Agustín, Félix, and I all piled into the same Lada
that brought us to the party, deciding to head back to my hotel for
a late night drink – not that they hadn't had enough booze - before
calling an end to the predawn adventures. Fortunately, these cute
boys held their liquor well.

At this particular hotel, native guests could come into the lobby after a thorough visual dressing down by the security guards, both plain-clothed and uniformed. But the *muchachos* were not to be stopped or intimidated. With me as the guest-card-carrying part of the entourage, we swept into the lobby and cozied up to the bar. Of course, everyone ordered more drinks, and of course, I paid for them. No discussion was necessary; this was my role. And besides, I was on vacation.

While we sat there in the nearly-deserted bar sipping and tripping, the bartender, a regular-looking middle-aged José pulled Agustín aside: "Does your friend want to take his friend upstairs?" Agustín then asked me directly, in front of everyone. The bartender, from the other side of the small bar, said, "It's vacation – while in Cuba, you should enjoy it."

I shrugged and looked at Félix. "Do you want to go?"

"Sure." He replied nonchalantly.

The bartender nodded and told us to chat and drink for a moment. He motioned to the guard stationed next to the elevator, who trotted over, listed to the bartender, mumbled something in a low growl. The bartender came back and told us "give me $15 and your friend can go upstairs until the guard's shift ends in two hours." It was a few minutes before 5:00 a.m. "But your friend has to be gone by then." Everybody watched – Agustín, Diego, Abél, Félix – as I pulled the dollar bills out of the pouch I kept tucked in my front pocket and peeled off $15. I handed them to the bartender and looked over at Félix. He had a funny look on his face – not quite perturbed, not angry, and certainly not happy. Then I had second thoughts – "what did I just do? Pay the pimp?"

At any rate, we said our goodnights to the guys, who had to drink up and leave the hotel once I left the lobby. Félix and I got into the elevator and rode up to the room. I fumbled with the key in the lock. We were finally going to get to consummate this relationship. I was finally gonna get what I'd come all this way to get: my very own sample of the world famous Cuban pinga.

Cuba is a phallic country. Reminders are everywhere, from the fat and thick *plátanos* hanging from trees – peeled, sliced, fried, and served with *moros y cristianos* – to hand-rolled Cuban cigars – long, sleek, earth-brown and fragrant – to the shape of the country itself, rising slightly north in the west, like an early morning hard-on. Reminders were in the full-to-bursting baskets some fellows sported in tight jeans, or the delectable family jewels occasionally groped by lounging hands through cut-off shorts. *Pinga* was in the air. Félix's was like a long cone, thick at the base and more slender at the top, capped off by the mushroom glans peeking from under its hood. It stirred and flopped around like a drunken snake, just like its less-than-sober owner, who was somewhat uninterested in the whole scene. The early morning silence was punctuated only by the constant buzz of the overhead light and an occasional slide of skin against bare sheets. It was anticlimactic, to say the least. Then both of us fell asleep.

At 6:45 a.m., the phone's loud ring jarred me from sleep. The security guard from the lobby spoke softly but firmly: "It's time for your friend to go." I tried to rouse Félix, who refused to get up.

"That was the guard! He says you've got to go NOW. Get up! You're going to get in trouble!"

"No I won't. Don't worry about it," he replied, calm, stubborn, and still half asleep. I didn't know whether they would arrest both of us or not, so I wasn't taking no for an answer. No way was I going to some rotten hellhole of a prison over a piece of dick that I didn't even enjoy! No, his ass was gonna get up and outta here. I pulled his arm and even tried pushing him off the sheets, but he kept saying "*no, no te preocupes*!" Only a few minutes later, as I grew tired of tugging and pleading, there was an insistent knock on the door. That got his attention – Félix sat right up in bed and started scrambling for his clothes. I could hear my heart pounding through my ears as I approached the door, suddenly furious and regretful that I'd gone through with the whole thing, as a vision flashed through my mind of my mother visiting me in a Havana jail, her saying "Well what were you thinking? All of this for some sex?"

The guard wasn't taking any risks, nor was he taking no for an answer. He came upstairs to personally escort Félix out of the hotel before his shift ended and before Félix's stubbornness got us all in trouble.

VI.

He loves me. He loves me not. He loves me?

Él me ama:

los besos. Las cartas. Las palabras. Kisses. Letters. Words.

Él no me ama:

borracho. Cabezudo. Drunk & stubborn.

Pero

él me ama.

I recall
Mi querer.
Mi vida.
Mi cielo.
Mi fresa y chocolate.

Él me ama.

VII.

¿Me amas?

I was nervous about meeting his mother, Señora Silvia. Félix led me through their neighborhood, a neglected section of Centro Habana that reeked of stagnant water and rotting garbage. Their apartment was two stories up, in the back of what was probably once a grand mansion built around a courtyard. The courtyard still existed, with laundry lines strung from one side to another. The building had been carved into smaller apartment units for a multitude of families, judging from the kids running around and squealing with glee. Initially I was concerned about the near decrepit physical state of the building, much like many of the places I'd seen in Havana, with steps missing, walls peeling, and bare light bulbs hanging. With makeshift repairs in place, the residents went on living the best they could under the circumstances. This seemed to be the general way of operating: do what you can to get by with some dignity.

I always judge a man's character by his relationship with his family. Just like me, Félix was close to his mother and didn't talk much about his absent father. That was a good-enough sign. La Señora greeted me warmly with a broad smile, outstretched arms, and a kiss on each cheek, European style. I wondered if she knew that her son and I were more than casual pen pals, but I returned her warmth with an appreciative hug of my own. La Señora seemed young to be the mother of two adults, having given birth to Félix when she was 17 and to another child when she was 30. I never got to meet Yuliana, his 19-year-old sister, because she'd married a Spaniard and was whisked away to live in Sevilla, leaving behind her own cute three year old son to the care of her mother, Félix, and a stepfather not much older than Félix. La Señora had a youthful spirit and, the few times that I saw her, was always dressed and groomed to a T – hair pressed and slicked back into a short ponytail, shirts and skirts ironed and neatly tucked in, shoes cleaned with a wet rag every day. Her face was unlined and complemented by light makeup. She looked like a still, hot cup of coffee with a dab of milk – brown and smooth. She smiled easily and spoke nicely, though I could barely understand what she had to say because of her accent and the speed of her speech: "*Buenotheea micarino, muchogutoenencontrart.*" I'd always look over to Félix for a translation at a slower clip, one that my still-foreign ears could understand.

Like Señora Silvia, their apartment was sunny and neat. I especially took note of the altar sitting on a small table in the corner of the living room. It was adorned with a white candle, several multicoloured beaded necklaces representing various Orishas and a brown baby doll dressed in lacy white ruffles and a headwrap like a Santera. Walking through the tiny galley-style kitchen, Félix guided me up a ladder to the sleeping quarters in an attic-like space underneath the building's rafters. Two mattresses lay flat on the floor. I wondered how they found any privacy, particularly for intimate moments.

The second time I visited them at home, Señora Silvia again greeted me familiarly and asked if I wanted anything to drink or eat, not that they had much to offer. She and Félix went into the kitchen and chatted quietly for a minute, then he came back into the living room with me.

"*Tesoro*, can you give my mother $20 for an iron? Her iron broke and she needs a new one. That way she can take in other people's laundry so she can make some money on the side. Especially to help out with Luís' expenses." Luís was Félix's nephew. Señora Silvia listened from the kitchen door. "It's just $20." How could I say no, the "rich" *norteamericano* who sent money down to them every month? How could I say no sitting in her living room after she'd been so nice to me before, genuinely, so I thought? Félix put his hand on my shoulder. "It would help us so much." The Señora, probably sensing some of my discomfort, stepped back into the kitchen while Félix pressed in for the close. "Do it for me," he said in a near-whisper, kissing me on the cheek while his mother was safely in the kitchen banging pots and pans.

"Oh all right." I was pissed. I was on a strict budget while in Havana and knew that this would cut into my per diem that I had set aside for both of our expenses, since I was paying for everything. I took out the little pouch tucked in my front pocket that held my greenbacks – I didn't carry any Cuban money the entire time I was there – and unfolded a twenty. Félix called his mother, who came and stood in the kitchen doorway wiping her soapy hands. I tried to hand the money to him.

"Give it to her," he quietly ordered.

"No, you asked for it, you take it. Here."

"No, give it to her. This is a gift for her, not me."

Had my command of Spanish been good enough while mad, I would've said "I thought I was doing it for you." But I never think of the good comebacks until later.

I handed the folded bill to the Señora, who snatched it – as politely as one can snatch anything – and added *"Gracias"* wearing either an embarrassed smile or a smirk. *¿Como se dice* "sucker"?

nadie
podrá
quitarnos
la esperanza

Me ama.

His eyes became mine. He was my official unofficial tour guide, leading me around the grid of Habana Vieja streets. Tourists wove in and out of the historic quarter's restaurants, bars, and galleries, shoulder-to-shoulder with the local citizens trying to supplement their state-approved jobs with extra gigs to earn crisp greenbacks. We rode a cocotaxi—a glorified motorcar with a bright orange shell, through central Habana close to his family's apartment. We posed for pictures in front of the beautiful baroque Catedral de San Cristóbal, where the remains of Christopher Colombus once lay before being returned to Spain. Félix treated me with tickets to a performance of the National Ballet at the awe-inspiring Gran Teatro de La Habana, whose grandeur setting rivaled any of the precisely choreographed action onstage.

At my request he took me to a barbershop, basically a few stools in an old storefront, where, like cut shops in the States, the barber argued with and teased his clients, whipping out sharp cuts with his electric razor steadily buzzing. The barber, a slender thirty-something wearing a tight red lycra shirt, jeans and a thick chain, asked me where I'm from, noting that my face is "rounder than a Cuban one" so he knew I was from somewhere else. Afterwards, away from the shop, Félix stroked the outline of my face, approving my shape up and trim: *"que cara linda. Cabello nuevo, cara linda."* New hair, beautiful face.

Later we entered his neighborhood church where he lit a candle for the Virgen de la Caridad del Cobre, Cuba's matron saint. Then he knelt and crossed himself, whispering prayers and mantras. The Virgen has an alter ego in Ochun, the Yoruba orisha of love and money. I immediately appreciated this bit of divine humor and alignment: this relationship between Félix and me seemed to teeter between love and money, the romantic and the transactional. He and I needed blessings from Ochun for both!

Learning more about the Orishas opened my eyes to the brilliance of Africans who maintained their divine connections under the guise of the enslavers' saints. European masters tried valiantly and violently to strip away every cultural norm of their African captives in order to assert European superiority as a twisted justification of the heinous institution of slavery. In spite of these all-out attempts to erase their humanity, Africans displayed a near-miraculous fortitude and cleverness in keeping their worship systems intact by adapting them to fit the colonizing religion, Roman Catholicism. This gave birth to Candomblé in Brasil and Santería in the Spanish-speaking Caribbean. Shango became Santa Barbara. Ogún was San Lazaro. Olodumare is represented by the long-haired Christ figure, and Yemanja, shrouded in her sea-blue glory, still looked over her human flock as the Virgin Mary. Félix and Señora Silvia recognized both schools of worship as valid ways of accessing the All-Knowing.

"We must pray all the time," Félix told me. Yes, we must.

Félix went to the front of the church to pray further and I sat in the back. I thought about Yemanya, seeing my own mother's face in the statue of a rich chocolate-skinned, chubby-cheeked mother deity, both a nurturer and a fierce warrior for the protection of her children. As a lapsed Christian, I was a mere observer in this realm, warmly curious about the Orishas, but struggling and hard-pressed to dispel the deep-seated suspicion of African spirituality bred by years of puritanical North American Christianity, where everything not "of Christ" was voodoo, black magic, nearly-naked heathens dancing wildly around fires in the jungle. Nevertheless, that day my plea was aimed at any force that would hear me: *Pleeeease God and Universe and Yemanya and Ochun and Cuba and Uncle Sam! I'm calling on everyone to make this relationship work!*

I wanted to be with Félix. I wanted him to be with me. I wanted us to be together, all the time and in the same location for as long as it could last. I wanted to test our relationship experiment in the opportunity-fertile ecosystem of the Golden State, where dreamers make their dreams come true. He desperately wanted to leave Cuba and I desperately wanted to help. So that he could be with me.

I was even willing to dance naked around a fire in the jungle.

So the dream was to host him in the United States. For the time being, we'd move into my studio apartment in the Mission and survive on my modest salary. He would take English classes at the City College three blocks away and bus tables at one of the many Valencia Street restaurants nearby while working toward his green card after applying for asylum. He would be covered by my health insurance. He would congregate at Radio Habana or The Ramp or Dance Mission with other Bay Area Cubanos displaced by unbearable politics and economics of *La Patria.* He would charm my friends one by one or en masse as they came to understand one another's accents and lives. They would fawn privately to me about how gorgeous he is and how he dotes on me. He and I would hike through the Marin Headlands together and gaze awestruck on the Golden Gate Bridge. We would try different tastes outside the paladares. We would eat soul food and *sofrito. Congrí* and collards. *Ñame* and yams. Red Velvet and

Ropa Vieja. We would send remittances to each of our mothers. And he would love me like no one had ever done before, take me to a place in love where I had never been. He would kidnap me with his caresses until they carried me above and beyond the moon in the diamond studded sky.

I believed it was possible.

ALMA MATER

IX.

Él me ama.

I am learning:

Tostones, fruta bomba, bacalao, congrí, lechón. Sotomayor, Stevenson, Savón. Eleggua, Siete Potencias, collares. Yambu, guanguanco, timba, son. Bamboleo, Los Van Van, Orisha. Claves, conga, tumbao. Regla, Guanabacoa, Santiago. Coppelia, Tropicola y Ron, Mi Cayito. Mulato, jabao, trigueño, chino, moro. Rojo, Blanco, Azul.

X.

In order to be able to spend some time together without having to dodge the distrusting gaze of hotel security or la Señora's movements around their apartment, I decided before my return trip to rent a *casa particular*, a private residence that the owner leased out, giving extra cash to its owner and some degree of privacy for its renters. Félix had befriended a gregarious woman who owned an extra place not far down the street from the University. Magdelena was slightly graying and had two children living in south Florida. From time to time, whenever she could get a visa, she would travel to the States and earn cash under the table by cleaning houses for a friend in Miami. She'd then take the cash back with her into Cuba and live for months at a time without working.

Magdelena's *casa particular* was cozy, but not without challenges. The toilet seat was missing. The shower was connected to a water heating gadget that threatened to electrocute the bather. There was little natural light available in the apartment, except through the bedroom window. The bedroom window shutters opened to a trashy backyard and the balcony of another building within spitting distance. This would later prove to be a nuisance when trying to get some fresh air while lying in bed.

When Magdelena took Félix and me to see the apartment, a couple of guys—a Cuban and a Canadian, were preparing to leave. Magdelena, evidently a local "friend of the gays," introduced all of us. The Cuban had just received his permission to leave, permiso de salir, from the Cuban government and would soon be living with his partner in the colder climes of Montréal. Since Canadian law at the time allowed for same-gender domestic partners to immigrate, this was yet another time that I wished that I were Canadian. Of course the Cuban was both excited and reluctant to depart sight unseen for a new land.

"I'm afraid it's going to be boring there. There's no music in the people there. What happens if I'm bored and cold?"

We all laughed, and I thought "But does it make a difference that you'll be bored, cold, and free?" Maybe not. Freedom at what price? Moving about in Cuba made me more thankful for my privilege of relative freedom, but maybe I didn't quite get the gravity of what it means to long for one's homeland, a place that one loves but can't flourish.

The lucky couple packed up and left. After seeing it, I agreed to rent the apartment, so Magdelena told us to come back in a few hours so that she could have time to clean the place. Félix and I agreed to go to our respective places and pack, then return to the casa, where we'd move in and begin celebrating our little mini-honeymoon. We'd buy food to cook in the tiny but neat kitchen before going to a party in the evening.

Later that afternoon, Magdelena directed me to sign two copies of a rental agreement and pay cash up front. Félix had packed three small bags full of clothes and toiletries, since he didn't own a suitcase and couldn't put everything in one bag. He was excited by the adventure of living away from home and perhaps by "playing house." But I couldn't have guessed what he was most excited about: going to the grocery store!

Up the street from the apartment building was a small basement grocery store, one that reminded me of markets I'd seen in D.C. brownstones. This was a dollar store, so it was well-stocked with items from Latin America and Europe. Payable in dollars, of course. To Félix, it was like entering heaven. I could only imagine what he would be like at Safeway at home, where the sheer number of choices can even boggle my mind!

While walking through the aisles of the store, we played grocery tug-of-war over things that he wanted but I didn't. "What about this? These are *muy sabroso*," he'd say, pulling some random item off the shelves or out of the freezer. I'd brought a limited amount of money with me from the hotel safe, and didn't plan to go back for more, so I kept cautioning Félix that we had to spend wisely. We ended up with an assortment of food for the next few days of our apartment adventure – eggs, bread, milk, spaghetti, hot dogs (he refused to be without meat), beer (which I don't drink), mango juice (potentially soothing to my stomach), cookies, and a few vegetables for a salad of some sort. Surprisingly, we didn't buy any rice, beans, or plátanos, all Cuban dinner staples. Maybe he wanted a change of pace.

Back in the apartment, as we were putting the food away, Félix became more playful, getting over the pout he'd put on in the grocery store when I kept saying "no" to things he'd point out like pickled eggs and pressed fruit strips. He'd pat me on the ass or press his considerable crotch into my rump. At one point he turned me around, leaned me against the refrigerator, and slid his tongue into my mouth. He pulled out of the deep kiss, smiled, and went into another room.

I finished stacking the vegetables on the counter for later use, and put a pot of water on the stove to boil. Félix called to me from the bedroom. "*Ven aca*." Come here.

When I walked into the room, he was lying on the bed, magnificently naked, with his legs spread wide, fully aroused. Ven aca.

I hadn't remembered his body to be so beautiful, especially his chest of wide and taut pecs. His arms and shoulders were the enviable sort that people at my gym spend hours trying to build up, thick and bundled like the carved wood of a large table leg. I could hardly believe this was all for me. I slid onto the bed and straddled him, kissing and caressing all the while. He pulled at my shirt, taking it off over my head while I moved further down his body, sucking his chocolate-kiss nipples, licking his underarms, and nibbling his treasure trail. I'd just reached further south when somebody banged on the door, making us both jump.

"Fumigación!"

Félix rolled out of bed and grabbed his pants, muttering and cursing. "We have to leave the building for 15 minutes while they spray for bugs. Turn the water off and put the food in the refrigerator."

We left the apartment, both blue-balled, as the other residents filed out of the building. Two young women held clipboards and wore matching dark grey uniforms, watching everyone leave. The hundred or so residents of the building stood outside, much like folks do during a fire drill, while young men with big canisters of bug spray walked into the building to set off the debugger bombs. Since we wouldn't be able to re-enter the apartment for at least twenty minutes, Félix said, we walked down the street to a little square and sat underneath a sprawling tree.

My stomach was turning flips when we returned to the casa particular. The fumigation had unsurprisingly left a heavy pesticide scent all throughout the building. We opened all the windows in the apartment, hoping to catch some sort of cleansing breeze, but that didn't work. Félix started coughing, which lasted throughout the night, a deep, bronchitis-sounding hack sounding like his body was trying to fight its way up through his throat. So between my nausea, which was magnified by the sharp and heavy pesticide scent, and his cough, we ended up tossing out any other entertainment plans for the evening and stayed in. We slept spoon-style with me holding him while he spasmed through the night.

The day after the fumigation, I came back to the apartment after my class at the Universidad and Félix handed me several sheets of paper with a red Maple leaf stamped across the top.

"I went to the Canadian consulate to find out about immigration. I need to get a letter of invitation so that I can get my visa."

One of the documents outlined the requirements for travel to Canada by Cuban nationals. I knew a few people in Canada, but what Félix was suggesting was that he travel there in order to get married. "If I have a letter of invitation from una chica in Canada, then I go up there and cross the border and we'll be together. Or she'll marry me and we'll live together, she with her girlfriend and me with you. In separate bedrooms, of course."

He asked me if I knew any single Canadian women, particularly lesbians. I wasn't sure what the deal was in Canada, but I know that in the States, many people consider marriages of convenience as more of a hassle than they are worth. My ex-boyfriend had married a woman from abroad so that she could stay in the States with her girlfriend and their infant daughter; after two years, she would receive a green card and they would get a divorce. I didn't think this woman was particularly nice or gracious, and she always seemed to be picking fights and screaming. I used to tell him that he needed to put little green index cards all around the apartment, so whenever she started some shit all he would have to do is tear up one of those green cards kept nearby and that would silence her. But he never did that.

Despite the vaunted free education and high literacy rate in Cuba, Félix's handwriting was elementary, almost childish, for a high-school educated man of 31. I offered to write the application for him, but he countered with "If they ask me to write anything and see that the handwriting is different, they'll see that someone else did it and then they won't give me the visa."

I had no legal grounds for bringing Félix to the United States. Gay marriage, gay immigration, even gay sex itself was illegal in most, if not all, of the nation. Nevertheless, I still wanted to see what options might be left through Uncle Sam.

The U.S. Interests Section building sat bold and defiant on the Malecon, perhaps the best-maintained and certainly the most heavily-fortified structure along the seafront. It served in lieu of an embassy since official diplomatic relations between the U.S. and Cuba hadn't existed in 40 years. Throngs of people hung around outside, keeping a respectable distance from the military men surrounding the premises. I wondered if they were native guards hired to keep local citizens from storming the place and asking for asylum, as they had done with the Peruvian Embassy in 1980, precipitating the Mariel boatlift, an exodus of 20,000 Cubans by sea.

I wasn't sure that Félix was correct when he told me that the lottery had already passed to be considered for a visa in two years. "Two years? Why are they doing it so far in advance?" Nevertheless, my charge was to go inside and get information on what documentation was required in order for a Cuban citizen to marry an American and to get a visa.

As I approached the building, one of the beret-wearing gun-toters approached me, barking "Where are you going?" I pulled out my small blue booklet with an eagle clutching the olive branch and the arrows etched on the front. When he caught the gold insignia on the cover of my passport, he pointed me, with the barrel of his high-powered gun, to the first of several checkpoints as an entrance. The two female guards inside were very courteous and efficient. One told me that I needed to leave my passport with them. *I think not!!* No way was I leaving my blue shield behind. No way. She relented and allowed me to pass.

Most of the people in the waiting area were milling around, waiting to get visas or immigration-related information. In 1994, after a big exodus of balseros – rafters hoping to cross the Florida Straits on dinky floating contraptions – Castro and Clinton struck a deal that would allow a certain number of Cubans to emigrate to the U.S. each year in exchange for the return of any Cubans apprehended at sea. The definition of "at sea" was called into question when a south Florida camera crew filmed a zealous Coast Guard agent tackling a skinny, obviously unthreatening balsero in the Florida surf and causing an uproar in the Cuban exile community. Since the balsero was able to stand, advocates argued that he was technically on land, while the agent in question defined "land" as being out of the water. Most of these Cubans in the waiting room were choosing to emigrate the legal, dry way – their entry would be through a jet way, and would hopefully be much less traumatic.

When my number was called, I went to the window and spoke with a reserved-looking Señora with streaks of grey in her neat hair. I asked her what documentation was needed for a Cuban citizen who wanted to marry a U.S. citizen. "I'm here on behalf of my sister, who is interested in marrying a Cuban man."

"Just any Cuban man?" I couldn't tell if she was joking.

"No, a man she met when she was here last year. They have been corresponding for six months. He's waiting for me outside."

The Señora wrote out a list of requirements. "The process can take a long time, so be prepared. Even if they are married here in Cuba, they will need to get approval from U.S. authorities before he will be allowed to leave the country."
"*Muchas grácias, Señora.*"

I had no idea how we were going to pull this off, especially not in any short period of time. Not only would we need to find this imaginary sister/fiancée, we'd also need to prove that the two had met, show a track record of correspondence, get a marriage license and a permit to leave from the Cuban government, secure a visa to the United States, and show all of this other proof of a legitimate marriage between Félix and the TBD bride. *Marry her so you can be with me.* All of this so that he and I could live together in unsanctioned, unmarried bliss...or something. No way was it going to work. Desperation and so-called love, a terrible, combustible combination, drives people to attempt crazy things, across borders and against international policies. All this effort expended for the promise of dedicated companionship. And sex. Something akin to the love and relationships I'd enviously and repeatedly watched others enjoy. Sure, I recognized the absurdity of my situation while standing here in the air-conditioned fortress of the not-embassy: I wasn't just taking the road less traveled; I was on a barely-marked footpath in danger of losing my way.

Alas, I wasn't going to give up yet. We could continue to hope and "pray all the time."

El
Coppelia

XI.

¿Me amas? ¿Me quieres?

He wanted me. He paid attention to me. He knew that keeping me reasonably happy was part of his duty in our unspoken agreement – especially if he wanted to get out of Cuba. I was his link to a certain freedom. Once after we'd had sweaty, slippery sex on a morning that warned of unbearable heat and humidity, he asked me if I was satisfied. I wasn't. That's the problem with having a macho top for a lover. When I said no, he was shocked. I had to get out of bed, fish the dictionary from my bag, and look up the words "to lick" – *lamer*, and "to bite" – *morder*, so I could tell him, "*lames, no me muerdes.*" Learning his lesson, he pushed me back down on the bed and went back to work until I was satisfied.

Sí, te quiero.

He is less romantic, less enchanted than I am about our brown-skin-on-brown-skin reverie, our growing connection across the diaspora. Our ancestors ended up in the New World in the same way, surviving a horrific kidnapping, wrenching transatlantic passage, enslavement, dehumanization, and poverty. But unlike me, he understands that the national culture *is* his culture, that there is no Cuba without the African contributions to it. This is starkly different from the U.S., which still too often thinks of itself as a European nation, one that suffocates other nationalities in the name of the melting pot, one that keeps a superficial acknowledgment of our immigrant roots that belies a larger demand for assimilation. But Africa survives here nonetheless.

For me, our togetherness is nourishment. An affirmation. *Él me ama y le amo a él.*

XII.

On an evening of a gorgeous golden twilight, we took a cab through the tunnel under the bay to the Fortaleza de San Carlos de la Cabaña, a large fortress on the eastern bank of the Bay of Havana. It was built as part of the 18th century Spanish defense system when Cuba was the crown jewel in the Spanish colonial crown. Each night at 9 p.m. a sentry dressed in period costume performed a cannon firing ceremony to mark the closing of the city gates. The lights of the city twinkled peacefully in the distance, underneath an equally starry sky. After the *cañonazo* ceremony, a group of fierce rumba dancers gave a true show under the spotlights and decorative torchlight. I loved watching the men and women sparring in this charming, flirty, ritual-as-dance. On the sidelines, Félix tried to show me how to rumba, locking his arms in L-shapes and gyrating his shoulders with the drums. Soon the dancers went into the crowd to pull out unwilling or unwitting spectators. I pride myself on being a pretty good dancer, but the *rumbera* who grabbed my wrist made me look like a thrashing gringo fool. At least I kept time to the ferocious rumba beat. I loved it!

After the noise and fireworks of the *cañonazo* ceremony, a thick quiet settled over us. The very real toll of this long distance connection was ringing true again, despite our enjoyment of the two weeks of togetherness we'd just had, and annoyance at its brevity. Alone behind the locked doors of the casa particular, Félix lit a candle, paying careful attention to the direction in which the shadows were cast, aware of the risk of someone paying too much attention to our silhouettes. We undressed in the silence, almost as though we were just getting ready for bed.

Once completely nude, Félix stood in front of me. A silver shimmer from the candlelight was refracted off the chocolate tint of his skin. I felt self-conscious standing naked in front of him because he was so beautiful, but took my cue from watching the arc of his arousal, which triggered my own. Yes, he was beautiful. I wanted to lick the satin sheen of sweat from his brown and golden body. I wanted to taste him, to re-taste the rum-flavored mouth, the combination of Tropicola and flesh. I wanted him to taste me. He ran his hot velvet hands over my skin, which tingled at every point of contact. He gripped the back of my neck and pulled me to his face, kissing me deeply, moving our heads in slow circles. The sensation of our lips meeting then recessing, meeting then recessing, made me swoon. He set out to find every epidermal erogenous zone on my neck, sucking with varying degrees of pressure, making me writhe as pleasure ran up and down my spine. He pressed himself against my backside, continuing to kiss my neck and rub my chest, encircling and pinching my nipples. I ground my hips against his hardness and we found a joint rhythm. In silence. We stroked contours and tasted crevices. This was like dreaming, a sensation of time within time, where the perception and the reality of time detach from one another.

That night, we were setting aside the truth about this highly-charged lovemaking; it was a goodbye ritual, a goodbye with an uncertain future behind it. We both knew that this would be our last coupling for a while, maybe forever – I was leaving the next day. That night, I opened myself completely: I wanted him to possess me, to become part of me, deep inside. I wanted him to envelop me with strong arms and protect me from the ugliness of solitude. I wanted him to fight for me, to fight to be with me, to fight together. I wanted to know every inch of him, for him to have intimate knowledge of my body and mind so that there was nothing left to hide. I wanted his life serum, his seed, knowing that the only procreation possible was the rekindling of my own life. I wanted him to love me thoroughly, unlike anyone else has ever done, so much so that his love was a shroud, a cloak, a tarp, a security blanket against everything that came before telling me that I was ugly, that I was skinny, that I was unsophisticated, that I was too black, that I was big lipped, that I was crooked teethed, that I had pimply bad skin, that I was too effeminate, that I was unappealing, that I was less than worthy of attention. Against every white insult and black rebuff. I wanted his love to be that powerful. I wanted to possess him, to run through his bloodstream like the lifestuff itself. I wanted to rule his head and heart so he would think of and feel me every day as if I were a phantom twin. I wanted to live inside of him until we could reunite again in person. I wanted our two to become one. This was not to be mere fucking; I wanted alchemy, fusion.

Our fit was so natural and easy this time that, seconds after the friction began, Félix caressed my face with his hand and kissed me softly, thoughtfully, on the lips. *Te amo.* My head was reeling from our push-pull dance of joy and desperation, uncertainty and trust, wanting it all but wanting to stop altogether.

Félix went over the top first, tonguing me more deeply as he did, the pistons in his hips grinding to a slow halt. My own climax radiated from my groin like a starburst, then crashed like sea waves against the Malecón wall. We coupled again and again, trying against hope to achieve the oneness that eluded us. In the deep hours of the night, we lay entangled, sweaty, and exhausted, as the implications of our separation bellowed through the silence. Tomorrow was the beginning of our future.

XIII.

28 de enero

i know that you feel desperate but don't worry because i will keep loving you. *bueno mi amor,* i will tell you that i fixed my teeth – it went very well and i am very thankful to you. okay, you will see little by little. *mi tesoro, saludos* to your mother and friends. don't feel depressed. i love you and want you and adore you very much. my mother sends greetings and hopes you are well.

until soon,
tu lobo

5 de feb
querido amor,
i am here every day in cuba with a great longing since you left for your country. i was very happy with you here giving your love. destiny separated us but i am sure that someday we will be together.

mi amor, i hope the days fly by because (as you know) i want to see you again but i understand that you have to work.

mi cielo, as soon as you're able, if it is within your means could you send me $50? like i explained to you, i want to repair my room in my apartment since whenever it rains my bed and clothes gets wet from the hole in the roof. you can understand this since you have seen this with your own eyes.

i don't have money to write you like i want because i have to buy a phone card for the computer for five dollars. i also ask that if you can, please send money for us to be able to communicate more and more.

i love you much and promise you that i won't forget you since i love you and i hope i showed it during those moments when we were together and happy.

my mother and nephew send *saludo* and hope that you are well. please send the money before February 15 and i will be very thankful to you and will wait anxiously for you. a million kisses. take care. *te quiero.*

chao,
tu lobito

7 de feb
hola mi amor. hope all is well with you. i got your message that a friend is possibly coming to cuba and i'm happy that we will be able to communicate. i send a letter by the mail but that isn't important. what is important is that it arrives in your hands since i am very anxious that you receive my messages.

remember that i was waiting to tell you a surprise at the end of the month? i got a visa to Russia! i am very nervous and happy. i once thought it couldn't be, but it may indeed happen and i am very anxious. as you know, i have to pay $400 to be able to travel. my sister is going to help with the air ticket. she's going to send me $1200. *mi amor,* i need your help now more than ever. this money that i have asked you for is for Cuban immigration – $300 for the immigration and $30 for the visa and $20 for the airport tax. my love, you don't have to send the entire $400, you can send $200 by 16 march and the other half by 16 april since i will travel the first week of may. please send the money on time so that i can go to immigration and start my departure from cuba. please tell your friends that we need their help. *bueno mi amor*, i love you and miss you. until the next time...

tu lobito

14 de feb
hola mi amor – i want to send you st. valentine's day greetings. here in cuba this is the day of lovers and is a very happy day for us. i want to give thanks to you because i received the money that you sent and now i can buy the materials to fix the roof like i told you about. i mailed another letter to you in order to save minutes since a phone card costs five dollars. well, you know. *mi cielo*, i must tell you that someone broke into our apartment and stole the vcr. my mother is very sad and nervous and we're looking for the thief.

bueno, i want to send a big kiss for your enchanting *nalgas* that are so marvelous and that i love to adore and another kiss for your sweet lips. my love i need you and you need me. i love you and don't forget. don't get with anyone else. *saludos* to your family and to your friend who was here in cuba and gifted me with a t-shirt and sneakers. for you, *mi amor*, a big kiss on all your body.

until soon,
tu lobo feros

23 de feb
mi amor i received your message and am very happy. i will tell you that i feel a bit of pain because here in cuba we have a cold freeze and a change of temperature and for this reason i have a little cold. but don't worry, it will pass. and the thief will also turn up someday.

mi amor, i am buying materials for the roof little by little. you asked me to buy a cd of the group we saw at the *café cultural.* if you send me the money, i will gladly buy it and send it with someone who can bring it to you. *bueno mi amor*, this is short because no time is left on the card. until next time, i love you and won't forget you.

8 de marzo
hola mi amor – todo bien. bueno mi cielo, don't worry - as soon as i receive all of the information and details of the trip i will tell you everything, ok. now i have to wait for permission from cuba and i will go on the 20th of this month to see if i can get the *permiso de salir t*o be able to leave cuba and as soon as the officials authorize my trip then i can get the ticket with the money that my sister will send.

mi tesoro, my mother and i waited saturday and sunday for your friend but she didn't come by our house like you said she would. i am very anxious to get this letter from you. if you had told me where she was staying, i could have gone to the hotel for the letter. *bueno*, that's not important, what is important is that i get this letter. ok. *bueno mi amor*, i desire you much and adore you every day. i am your love with a million kissesssssss. i love you!

tu lobito

19 de marzo
hola mi amor – ok i will tell you that i am very happy and thankful that i received your letter that you send with your friend nia. she was very friendly and charming and my mother and i were very happy with the photos that you sent. *mi cielo* today i will go to magdalena's house to share the photos with her and ask about the possibility of using her telephone to call you so that we can

talk and i can hear your beautiful and sweet voice that i love and always have by my side.

i will also tell you that i received the money ($225) that you sent together with the letter. *tu lobito* is very anxious to be close to your side to adore you and give you all the warmth that you need. i'm going to use a little to buy us food and a phone card and i will put this money in the bank until my departure so that i won't be able to touch it. this is only for my trip and i will save it better in the bank. *bueno mi querido* i won't say goodbye, only *adiós* and until the next letter.

tu lobito who loves you always

17 de abril
hola mi amor, i tried to call you this morning by telephone at Magdalena's house. Magdalena is in miami with her family right now and sends *saludos* to you.

MI AMOR – THIS IS VERY IMPORTANT! I NEED $2000 TO PAY FOR MY TRIP BECAUSE MY SISTER CAN NOT HELP ME WITH ALL OF THE EXPENSES! I BEG YOU TO ASK YOUR FRIENDS AND FAMILY TO HELP YOU TO HELP ME. I NEED THIS MONEY BY THE 27TH SO THAT I CAN BUY MY TICKET BY THE BEGINNING OF THE MONTH. PLEASE WRITE ME TO LET ME KNOW! *TE ADORO!*

27 de abril
hola mi amor. i hope you are well. *bueno mi cielo*, first i want to give you a million thanks for all of your help that you always give to me. for this reason i am always thankful to you, will always love and treasure you. please also thank your friends for being gener-ous enough to help with the money. i look forward to soon meet-

ing and knowing all of them and being able to thank them myself in person. on monday i will deposit the money in the bank until the hour of my departure arrives, and when it comes i will inform you of where you can find me and we can be together and very happy. ok, i love you most in the world and as soon as God desires, we will be together again. *muchos saludos* to all of your friends who have helped me and have supported our love and friendship. here on this small island there is a heart that loves and wants you. a million kisses on your body and your sweet mouth. i will never forget you.

tu lobito

1 de mayo
hola mi amor, todo bien. i send you warm greetings today, the day of the worker, for workers all over the world like you. *bueno mi tesoro*, everything is in order with my travel arrangements. on 21 may i will have all of my papers and i will tell you which day in june i will leave. my mother sends many kisses and hugs. i send you many kisses for you and your family whom i will soon meet. i love you and want to give you all or my love and caresses. very soon, my love. ok. *chao.*

tu lobito.

14 de junio
mi amor, do not worry about all of this money, i promise you that i will start working and will make all that i can make when i am there with you. do not worry. i won't want you to be upset and i understand, but this is the final and only chance that i have to leave. *mi amor*, my mother is also asking for this favor, she is here by my side asking for your help. she is crying and i am also because i might miss my flight if i don't have the *permiso de salir*

that i need from immigration. please ask your friends like jake and your boss who brought me the letter and all the others. this is the last opportunity that i will have. please do not be upset. do not lose confidence in me because when there is not trust between two people then the relationship dies. you know that i love you and need you and want to love you by your side, not from far away. my mother is very worried and has high blood pressure and is crying every day about the problems we have and don't know how to solve. if you can help me with $400 more dollars then i will find the $100 more that i need. please do what you can by the 29th or i will lose my ticket and this last chance to leave cuba so that we can be together and happy. when you send the money i will call you to give instructions on where i will be and how we can be together. *te amo.*

XIV.

If he is the *lobo*, am I the lamb?

XV.

If I were only writing from the end, the present, I would tell you that I still don't have an answer. Life offers few Hollywood endings, clear resolutions, and justice tied up with a bow.

If I had to buy love, buy adventure, so be it. Sometimes these things don't come easily to everyone. Earlier in my life I missed out on the late night sexual hijinks that seem to define "adventure." But because of Félix, I can no longer say that my life was flatlining in that respect. He brought me intrigue and mystery. There was passion and lust and hot sex. I do believe there was love, however convoluted it was. There may have even been deceit and pretense. Félix – and Cuba – changed me, made me more confident and open to possibilities, which literally lay around every corner. But this is with the benefit of hindsight.

Félix disappeared. Vanished with the money I sent him and the speck of our dream of living together here in the States.

Or maybe the dream was always mine alone.

After our last correspondence in June, Félix no longer returned my emails. I sent word to his mother through a traveler to Havana who hand-delivered a message to their apartment. La Señora wrote me multiple anxious pages of a letter in neat looping script, worried about her vanished son, worried about her family's economic situation. She knew he was going to leave, but for her own good Félix wouldn't tell her when or where he was going.

I started making up stories: was he really able to leave? Was he arrested at the airport and held in some hellhole? Had he been detained in some other country and deported back to Cuba? Had he, sick of waiting on the bureaucracy, climbed onto a homemade raft to tough it out on the high seas? Were he and his mom in cahoots, enjoying the short-lived benefits that cash brought to their household? Félix…?

Life moved forward around me. Sometimes I was in - and sometimes out - of its ebb and flow: promotions, births, milestones, blossoms. The world kept spinning. My hope for information, for a sign of Félix, faded with the passing of days. Every so often I think of him and wonder if he occasionally thinks of me, thinks of us, thinks of the promises he spelled out in letters that enticed me. But I let go and moved on. Had to if I wasn't going to end up like that reclusive great aunt holding the treasure box.

Remembering Félix is like viewing a sunset. It's moving to watch in motion, and then it's over, gone with finality, and the scene fades to black. But I'll always recall its heat, and I'm glad to have witnessed its beauty.

AFTERWORD

Since this story was first published, two landmark shifts have significantly altered the existing reality, placing *Eyes of Water & Stone* firmly into yesteryear. Marriage equality has become the law of the land – in theory if not in practice – in the United States. And under the leadership of presidents Barack Obama and Raúl Castro, the US and Cuba are moving carefully down a path toward normalized diplomatic relations. Hope is born anew with each change we encounter.

Yet, contemporary racial justice movements in the United States, largely galvanized in resistance to the police brutality and murder of African Americans, lead me to wonder what freedom really is and who is truly free. African-descended people in the US and Cuba face similar struggles within different contexts - limited economic opportunities, state-sanctioned harassment, lack of full political representation and enfranchisement, and the continued devaluation of African bodies.

We must pray all the time. And love ourselves. And resist oppression by insisting on our humanity. *Yes, we must.*

Cedric Brown
Oakland, CA
August 2015

www.ingramcontent.com/pod-product-compliance
Lightning Source LLC
Chambersburg PA
CBHW070342120726
47909CB00008B/2721